Diva Duck Goes to Hollywood

BY Janice Levy

ILLUSTRATED BY
Colleen Madden

Magic Wagon

visit us at www.abdopublishing.com

Published by Magic Wagon, a division of the ABDO Group, PO Box 398166,
Minneapolis, MN 55439. Copyright © 2013 by Abdo Consulting Group, Inc.
International copyrights reserved in all countries. All rights reserved. No part of this
book may be reproduced in any form without written permission from the publisher.

Looking Glass Library™ is a trademark and logo of Magic Wagon.

Printed in the United States of America, North Mankato, Minnesota.
052012
092012

♻ This book contains at least 10% recycled materials.

Written by Janice Levy
Illustrations by Colleen Madden
Edited by Stephanie Hedlund and Rochelle Baltzer
Cover and interior design by Jaime Lint

Library of Congress Cataloging-in-Publication Data

Levy, Janice.
  Diva Duck goes to Hollywood / by Janice Levy ; Illustrated by Colleen Madden.
    p. cm. – (Diva Duck)
  Summary: Diva Duck makes a splash in Hollywood, but discovers that sometimes
old friendships are best.
  ISBN 978-1-61641-887-8
  1. Ducks–Juvenile fiction. 2. Animals–Juvenile fiction. 3. Friendship–Juvenile fiction.
4. Fame–Juvenile fiction. (1. Ducks–Fiction. 2. Animals–Fiction. 3. Friendship–Fiction.
4. Fame–Fiction.) I. Madden, Colleen M., ill. II. Title.
  PZ7.L5832Div 2012
  (E)–dc23
                              2011051960

After traveling the world, Diva Duck and her friends were happy to return to the farm.

"Home, sweet home!" said the sheep.
"It's great to be baaa-ck."

"No more **mooo-ving** for me," said the cow.

"Oh my! Back in the sty!" said the pigs.

But, Diva Duck had other plans.

"Hollywood, here I come!" she said. "I'll make **new** friends. I am Diva Duck, destined for greatness!"

She left the farm and her old friends behind.

After Diva's concerts in Hollywood, crowds waited outside her dressing room. Everyone wanted a piece of duck.

Diva's new friends carried her bags.

They **like me**, *they* **really like me!**
Diva thought. *We'll be* **best friends forever.**

Each night Diva's new friends got the best seats in town. But one night, Diva's friends kept her out very late. She ate too much. She sang high and low.

"Party hearty!" said the fox.

The raccoon rubbed his paws. "Duck 'n' Donuts for everyone!"

By the time she got home,
Diva was too **pooped** to pop.

She forgot all about working out.

And she didn't practice her music.

At Diva's next concert, she **yawned** through her songs.

She forgot the words.
She sang off-key.
Diva's hips slipped.
Her knees knocked.

Her butt went boom-ducka-boom, then CRASH!

"The **duck's down!**" yelled Diva's fans.

Diva fled backstage,
looking for her friends.
But her dressing room
was empty. Diva
checked her messages.

"**Don't** caaawl us, we'll caaawl you," texted the crow.

"**Talk** to the paw," wrote the fox. "Nobody likes a **loser**."

The raccoon sent a picture of himself in disguise.

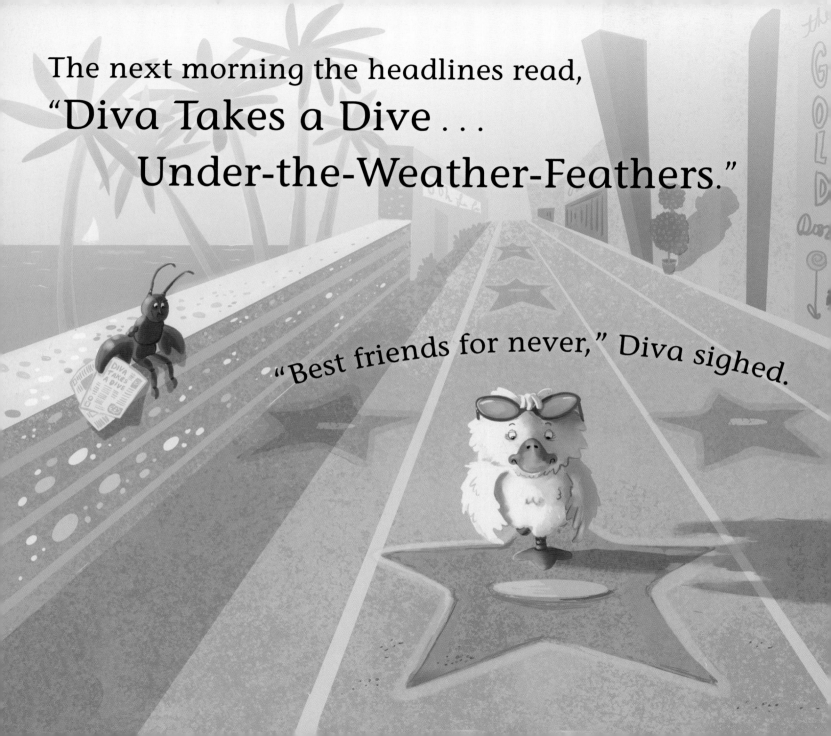

The next morning the headlines read, "Diva Takes a Dive . . . Under-the-Weather-Feathers."

"Best friends for never," Diva sighed.

Diva wandered the streets alone.
Her new friends were nowhere
to be found. The duck was
yesterday's news.

Word spread to Diva's old farm.
"Diva needs us," said the farmer. "Let's go."

Diva's **old** friends caught a flight to Hollywood. They found Diva in her pajamas eating a bowl of leftover fish.

The cows cleaned Diva up.
The hens cooked her a good meal.

"Best friends are forever," said the sheep.
"In good times and baaa-d."

"Really?" Diva sniffed.
"Of course," said the horse.
"Now, get to work."

Diva sang her scales.
She practiced her moves.
She mixed the beats.
She snapped out of
her foul mood.

"I am Diva Duck, destined for greatness," she said.

"I can dance. I can sing. I can do anything!"

That night, Diva jumped onstage and sang her feathers out. Her Little Quackers waved glow sticks and swayed.

"I'm baaaaaack!"

Diva yelled. And so are my *real* best friends forever!"

Diva's beak twitched.

Her hips swiveled.

Her butt went
boom-ducka-boom-ducka-boom-boom.

Diva Duck

⭐ Diva Duck followed her dreams and went to Hollywood alone. How did she make new friends?

⭐ Diva's new friends talked her into playing instead of working hard. What happened when Diva followed their lead?

⭐ Diva's true friends came back to help her. What would you do to help a friend in need?

About the Author: Janice Levy is the author of numerous award-winning children's books. Topics include bullying, multiculturalism, foster care, intergenerational relationships, and family values. She teaches creative writing at Hofstra University. Her adult fiction is widely published in magazines and anthologies.

About the Illustrator: Colleen Madden is an illustrator, mom, kickboxer, ukulele strummer, and honorary frog. She loves to draw for kids (and kids at heart!) and make people giggle. Diva Duck is her fourth series of children's books. She is currently writing her own titles as author/ illustrator, which will all be very silly books.